TO MARSHA ROTH

EZRA JACK KEATS
The Trip

GREENWILLOW BOOKS

A DIVISION OF WILLIAM MORROW & COMPANY, INC. · NEW YORK

Copyright © 1978 by Ezra Jack Keats. All rights reserved. No part of this book may be
reproduced or utilized in any form or by any means, electronic or mechanical, including
photocopying, recording or by any information storage and retrieval system, without
permission in writing from the Publisher. Inquiries should be addressed to Greenwillow Books,
1350 Avenue of the Americas, New York, NY 10019. Printed in U.S.A.   6 7 8 9 10

Library of Congress Cataloging in Publication Data   Keats, Ezra Jack.   The Trip.   [1. Halloween—Fiction]
I. Title. PZ7.K2253Tr   [E]   77-24907   ISBN 0-688-80123-4   ISBN 0-688-84123-6 lib. bdg.

Louie's family moved to a new neighborhood.
He didn't know anybody there.
No kids, no dogs, no cats.
And there weren't even any steps
in front of the door to sit on.
Louie sighed and went in.

He got an old shoebox.
He made a hole in the front,
cut out the back and part of the top,
and began to paste things inside.

He taped a piece of colored plastic on the top
of the box, and another piece on the end.
He hung his plane from the top, and closed the box.

Louie looked through the hole.

WOW!

Louie pretended he was flying his plane.
He flew higher and higher—over the moon.

He landed in his old
neighborhood.
It was very quiet.

He wandered around.
He could hear
his own footsteps.
Where was everybody?

He passed Roberto's old house—
and stopped suddenly.

He turned around
and ran—as fast
as he could.

He was trapped!

"Hey, wait—I know that tail!
It's the cat! And you're Roberto,
and that must be Amy and Archie."

They were his old friends!
"Surprise!" they yelled.
"Trick or treat!"

Louie took them for a ride
on his plane.
Everybody ran to the windows
to look at them.

It was time to go home.

Everyone was waving.

"Trick or treat!" Louie heard from far away.

"Come on, Louie," his mother was saying.
"Let me help you on with your costume."
They could hear the kids outside yelling,
"Trick or treat, trick or treat!"

Louie went outside
to join them.